Published By: Pen Legacy®
Interior Formatting and Illustration By: India Sheana

Library of Congress Cataloging – in- Publication Data has been applied for.

ISBN: 9781735142425

PRINTED IN THE UNITED STATES OF AMERICA.

DEDICATION

To my nephew KJ. May you grow up in a world that embraces your uniqueness, and loves you without condition. To all of my Black and Brown boys, and the parents and caretakers that are raising them, YOU MATTER!

~~I LO~~ve MY DAD.
HE'S SMART, TALL AND
STRONG. ALWAYS SMILING,
HE CAN DO NO WRONG.

EACH DAY HE WAKES ME WITH
MY FAVORITE SONG AND
SAYS, "SON, YOU MATTER!"

"I KNOW DAD" I SAY,
AS I EASE OUT OF BED, RUN
DOWN THE HALL. "SLOW
DOWN, SLEEPY HEAD!"

I BRUSH MY TEETH & WASH
MY FACE. "HURRY UP SON, WE
DON'T WANT TO BE LATE"

I RUSH DOWNSTAIRS TO GRAB MY FOOD, GIVE MOMMY A KISS, THEN WE'RE OFF TO SCHOOL. "HAVE A GOOD DAY", MOMMY SCREAMS. "I WILL, BECAUSE AFTER SCHOOL DAD'S TAKING ME FOR ICE CREAM!"

DAD WALKS ME TO SCHOOL WITH MY BAG IN HIS HAND, "REMEMBER AHMAD, BE A GOOD YOUNG MAN."

BE YOUR BEST, DO YOUR BEST AND DON'T GET CAUGHT IN THE CHATTER. BUT MOST OF ALL SON, REMEMBER YOU MATTER!

"I KNOW DAD" I SAY, AS I RUSH TO CLASS. HURRY ON THROUGH THE DAY, I JUST WANT TIME TO PASS. CAUSE I'M GETTING ICE CREAM AND I CAN'T WAIT. CHOCOLATE CHIP COOKIE DOUGH, THIS IS GONNA BE GREAT!

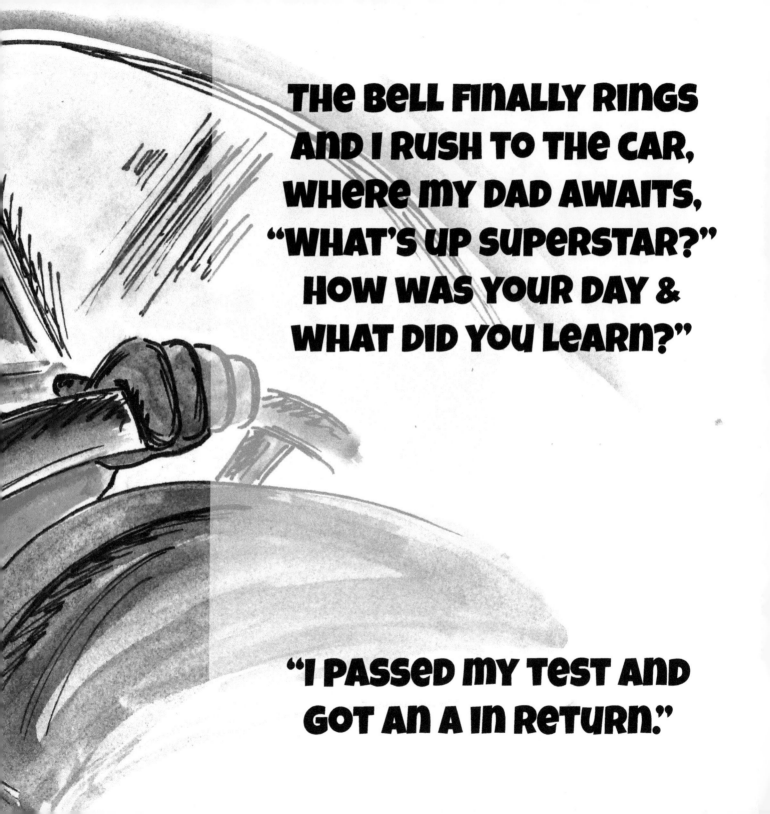

"THAT'S GREAT SON,"
AS WE DRIVE DOWN THE
STREET. LIGHTS FLASH,
THEN SIRENS BLAST AND
I TURN IN MY SEAT.

"PULL OVER THAT CAR!"
THE OFFICER YELLS!
DAD PULLS TO THE SIDE
AND PUTS HIS HANDS
ON THE WHEEL.

"AHMAD, FACE FORWARD AND YOU KEEP STILL, STAY CALM AND SIT BACK, IT'S OKAY JUST CHILL"

"WHAT SEEMS TO BE THE PROBLEM OFFICER, WHAT DID I DO?"

"STEP OUT OF THE VEHICLE, AND I'LL DEAL WITH YOU!"

DAD OPENS THE DOOR, AND THE OFFICER GRABS HIS GUN. "HEY MAN, CALM DOWN! DON'T DO THIS IN FRONT OF MY SON!"

"PUT YOUR HANDS IN THE AIR SO I CAN SEE THEM, OR I'LL SHOOT YOU RIGHT NOW. I DON'T EVEN NEED A REASON!"

"LEAVE MY DADDY ALONE!"
I YELL OUT IN FRIGHT!
"AHMAD BE QUIET SON,
IT'S GONNA BE ALRIGHT."

"WHOSE VEHICLE IS THIS?
WHO DOES IT BELONG TO?"

"HERE'S MY
REGISTRATION OFFICER,
LOOK I CAN SHOW YOU!"

"WELL WHY DIDN'T YOU SAY SO? I GUESS IT'S ALRIGHT. YOU TWO BE ON YOUR WAY AND HAVE A GOODNIGHT."

DAD GETS IN THE CAR AND WE DRIVE IN SILENCE. NO MUSIC, NO TALKING EVERYTHING IS JUST QUIET.

WE ARRIVE AT THE
PARLOR; DAD ORDERS
OUR ICE CREAM. THEN
WE SIT IN SILENCE, THIS
ALL FEELS LIKE A DREAM.

DAD HANGS HIS HEAD
AND LETS OUT A SIGH,
HE SNIFFLES A BIT AND
BEGINS TO CRY.

"AHMAD, NO MATTER HOW THEY TREAT YOU, NO MATTER WHAT THEY DO. REMEMBER YOU'RE A YOUNG BLACK KING, THEY CAN'T TAKE THAT FROM YOU!

STAY CALM AND LISTEN AND DO AS YOU'RE TOLD. I WANT YOU TO LIVE SON, YOU DON'T HAVE TO BE BOLD."

AS SOON AS HE SAID IT, HE BEGAN
TO WEEP. HIS ANGER, HIS SADNESS,
HIS PAIN WAS SO DEEP.

I SAT IN AMAZEMENT AND WATCHED
MY DAD. SO STRONG AND SO BRAVE,
YET NOW HIS SPIRIT WAS SO SAD.

I KNEW WHAT HE MEANT AND
WHY HE MUST'VE FELT SHATTERED.
SO, I GRABBED HIS HAND,
LOOKED HIM IN THE EYE AND SAID,
DAD, YOU MATTER!

CPSIA information can be obtained
at www.ICGtesting.com
Printed in the USA
JSHW022359110720
6627JS00002B/8